Lad

by Beth Reynolds
illustrated by Laura Freeman

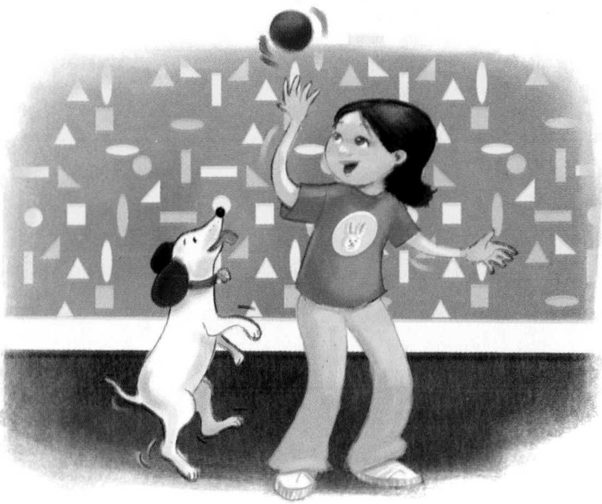

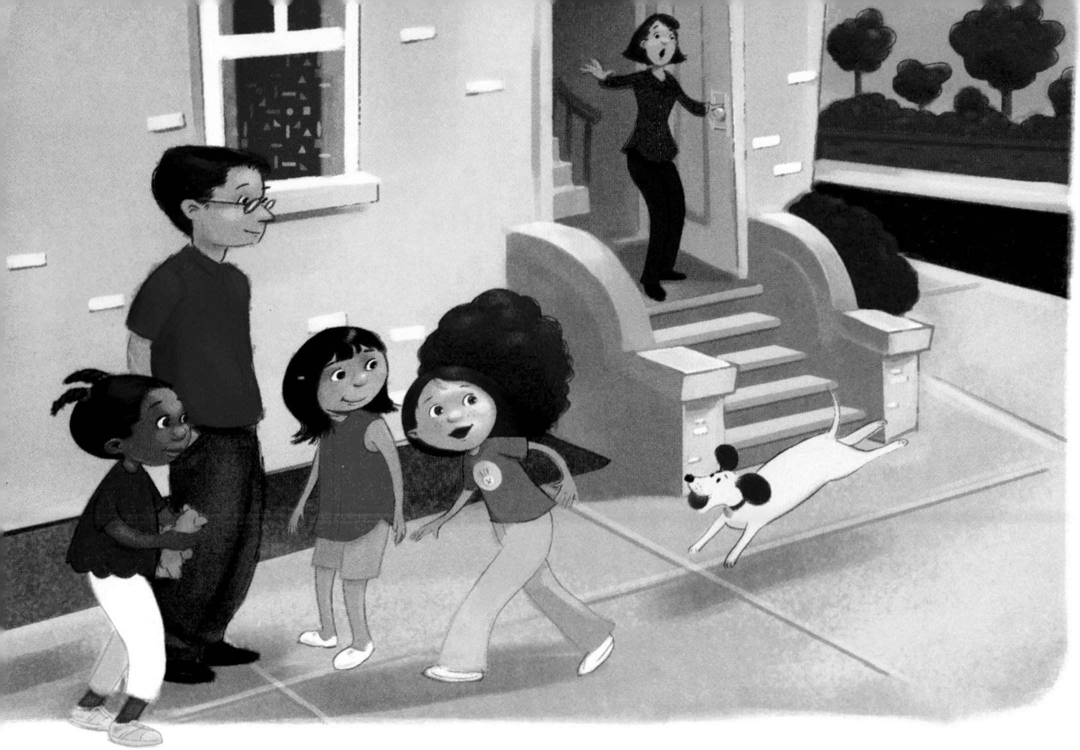

Kim can play.

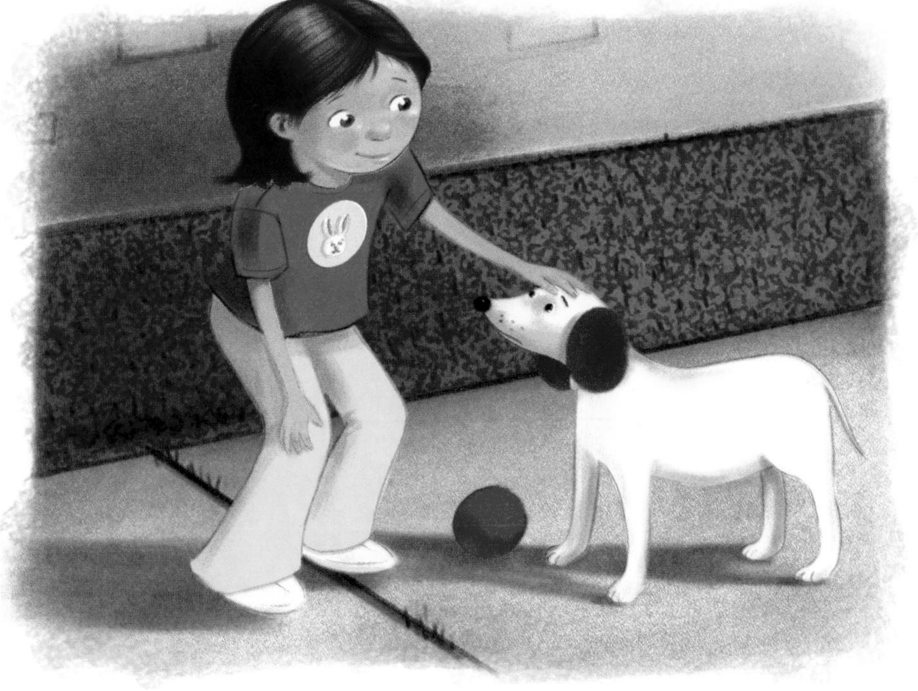

Lad can not play.

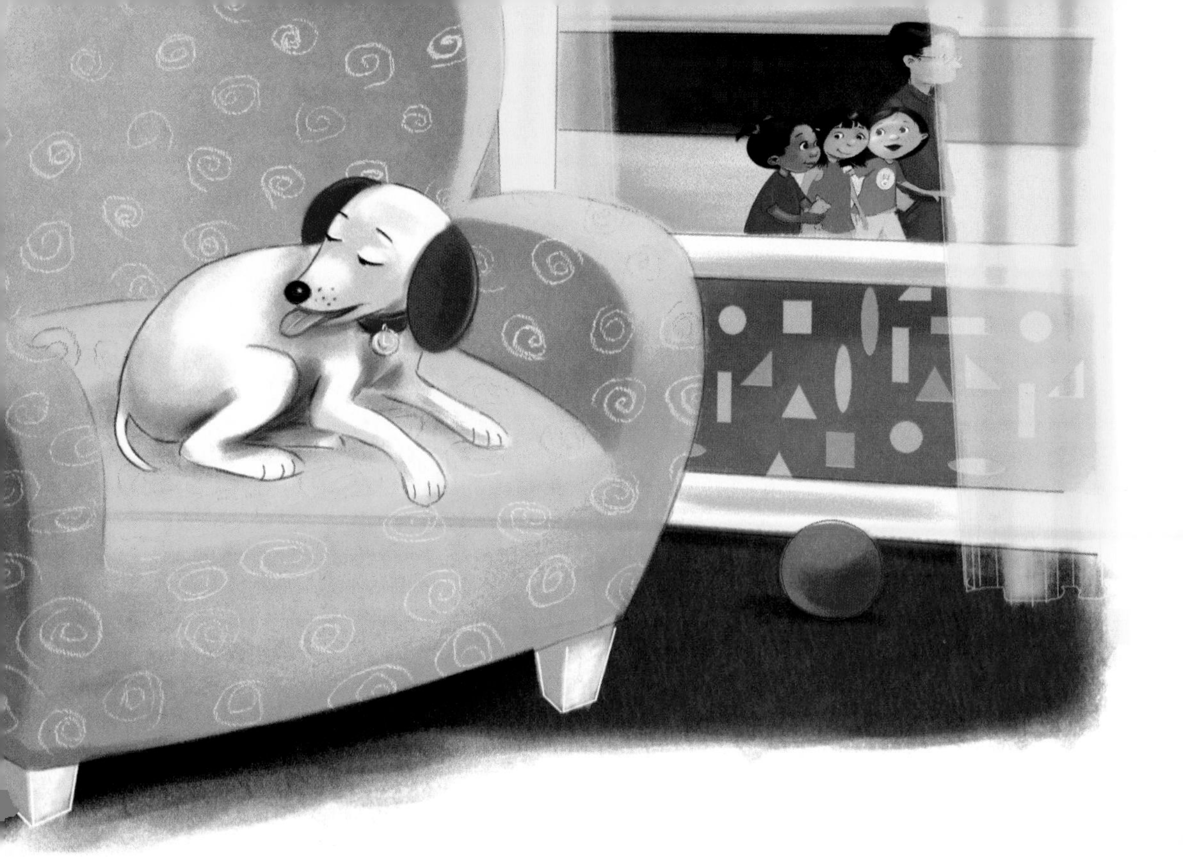

Lad can lick.

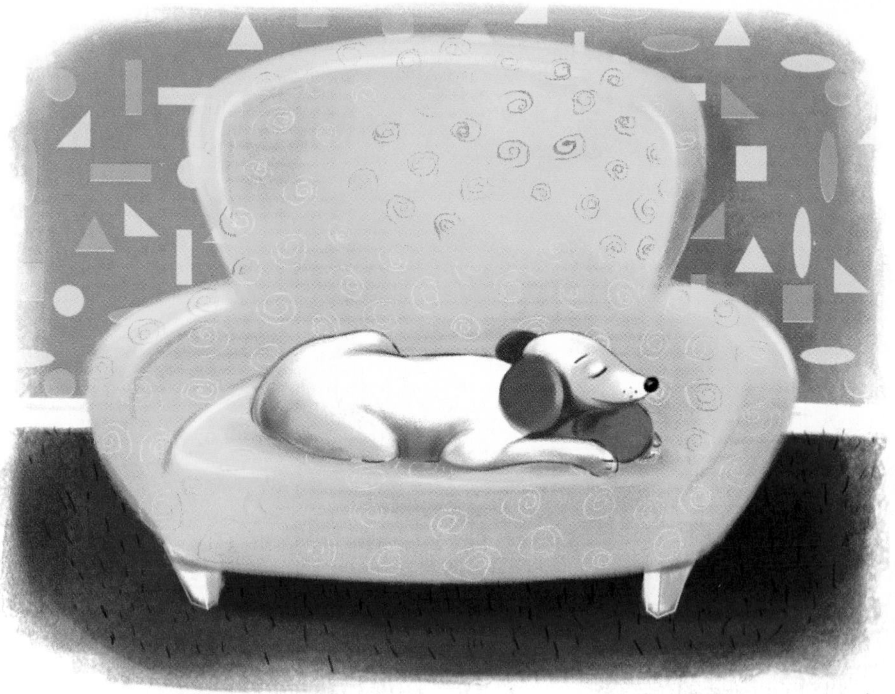

Lad can nap.

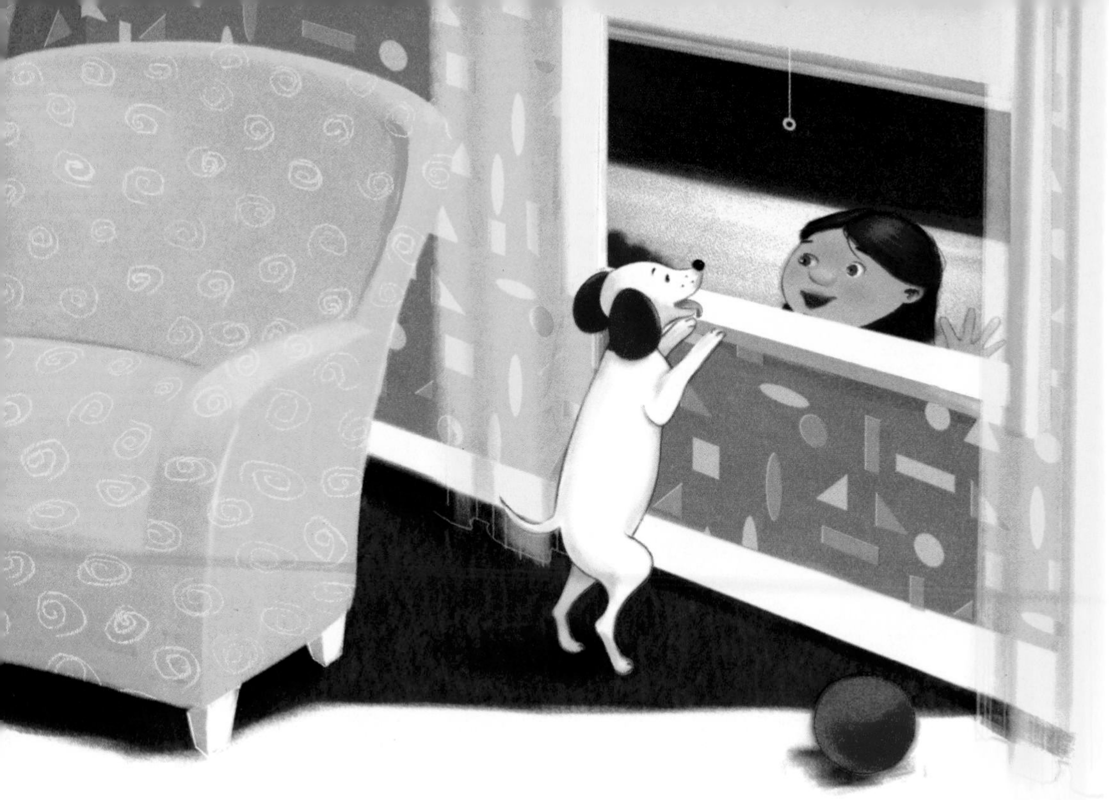

Lad can see Kim!

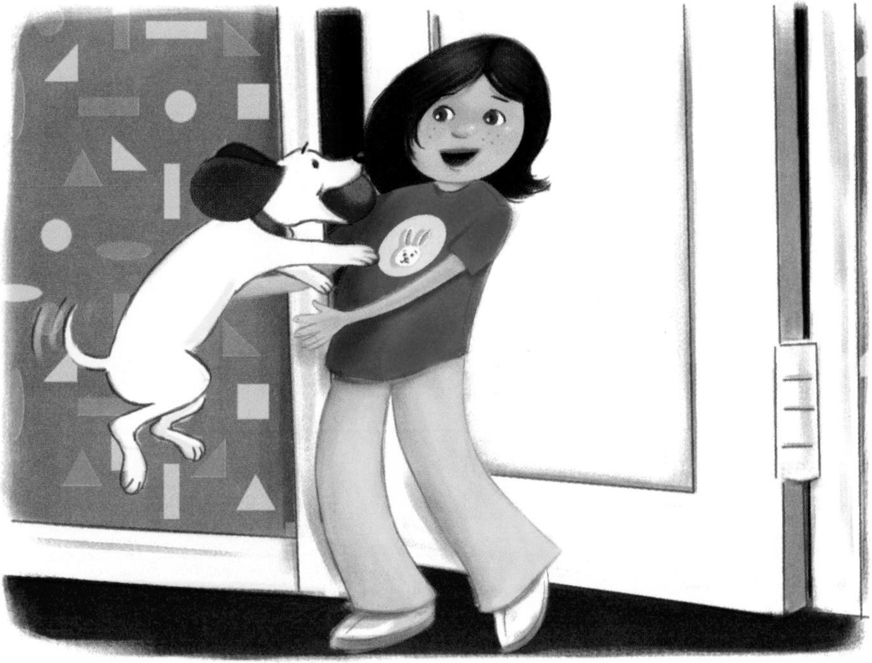

Lad can hop.

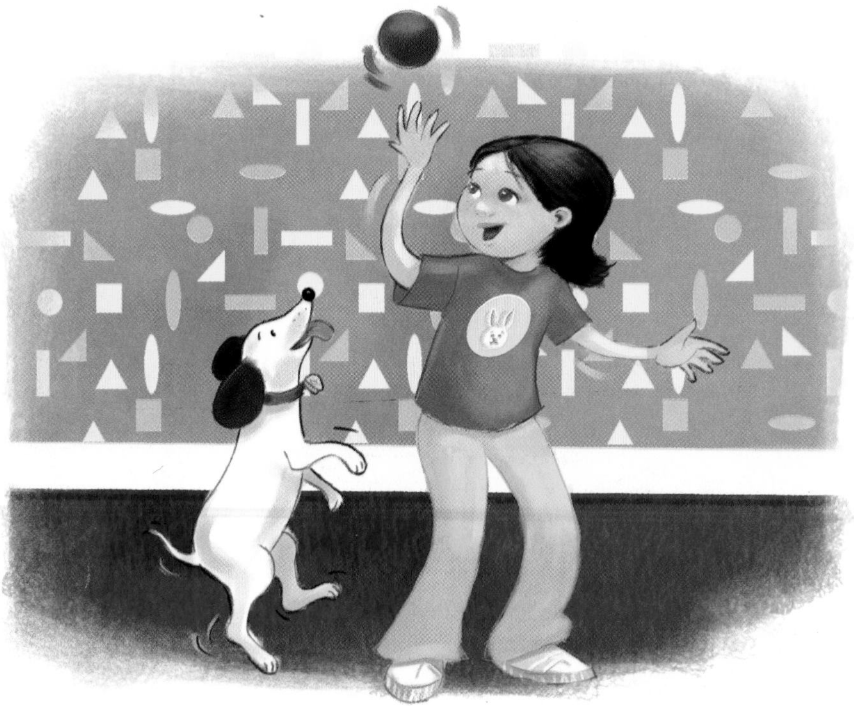

Lad can play!